I Could Catch a Whale
Yo Podría Pescar Una Ballena

By Pam Van Scoyoc
Illustrated by R.J. Lewis
Translated by Silvia R. Santillán-Cruz

By Grace Enterprises

A By Grace Enterprises Production

I Could Catch a Whale
Yo Podría Pescar Una Ballena
Text copyright © 2005 by Pam Van Scoyoc
Illustrations copyright © 2005 by By Grace Enterprises

Requests for permission to make copies of any part of this work should be sent to
By Grace Enterprises, 9515 Twin Oaks Drive, Manvel, Texas 77578, USA.
www.bygraceenterprises.com

First Edition

Cataloging-in-Publication Data

Van Scoyoc, Pam.
I Could Catch a Whale = Yo Podría Pescar Una Ballena / by Pam Van Scoyoc ; illustrated by R. J. Lewis ; translated by Silvia R. Santillán-Cruz.
p. cm.
English and Spanish
Summary: Andy wants to go fishing, but everyone is too busy to take him. His imagination takes him to a place where he is fishing and catches wondrous and magnificent sea creatures. Now, if only he could go fishing.
Audience: Ages 4-9
LCCN 2005920364
ISBN 0-9663629-5-0

1. Boys—Juvenile Fiction. 2. Fishing—Juvenile Fiction. [1. Boys—Fiction. 2. Fishing—Fiction. 3. Family—Fiction. 4. Family relationships—Fiction. 5. Sea Creatures—Fiction. 6. Rejection—Fiction. 7. Spanish language materials—Bilingual.] I. Santillán-Cruz, Silvia R.   II. Lewis, R. J.   III. Title. IV. Title: Podría pescar una ballena

PZ73.V 2005

Book layout by Emerald Phoenix Media
Cover design by Ira S. Van Scoyoc
Copy Edited by Shirin Wright
Printed in Hong Kong
Published in the USA

I Could Catch a Whale
Yo Podría Pescar Una Ballena

Dedications

Pam Van Scoyoc

To Bill, Jr., Bill, III, Ira, Lauchlan and Jonathan, the fishermen in my family who inspired this story, and can always find time to drop a line in the water.

A Bill, Jr., Bill III, Ira, Lauchlan y Jonathan, los pescadores en mi familia quienes han inspirado esta historia, y quienes siempre encuentran tiempo para tirar el anzuelo al agua.

R.J. Lewis

For my father, Sheridan C. Lewis and the beautiful Texas Gulf Coast, especially my hometown Corpus Christi.

Para mi padre, Sheridan C. Lewis y su hermosa Texas Gulf Coast, y especialmente, mi lugar de nacimiento Corpus Christi.

Silvia R. Santillán-Cruz

To my beloved parents, Eduardo and Pina, who always wished their offspring to learn at least two languages. Thank you from the bottom of my heart.

A mis amados padres, Eduardo y Pina, quienes siempre desearon que sus hijos aprendiéramos por lo menos dos idiomas. Gracias desde el fondo de mi corazón.

"If I could go fishing, I know I could catch a whale,"
said Andy.

"Sí pudiera ir de pesca, yo sé que yo podría pescar una
ballena," dijo Andy.

"I would take the longest pole in the whole wide world and catch the biggest whale in the ocean."

"Me llevaría la caña de pescar más larga de todo el mundo entero y pescaría la ballena más grande del océano."

"Daddy! Daddy! Can we go fishing?"

"¡Papi! ¡Papi! ¿Podemos ir de pesca?"

"Not today, Andy. I have to go to work."

"Hoy no, Andy. Tengo que ir a trabajar."

"If I could go fishing," said Andy, "I would use the sharpest fishhook in the whole wide world to catch a great white shark with long pointed teeth."

"Sí pudiera ir de pescar," dijo Andy, "usaría el anzuelo más afilado de todo el mundo entero y pescaría un enorme tiburón blanco con grandes dientes afilados."

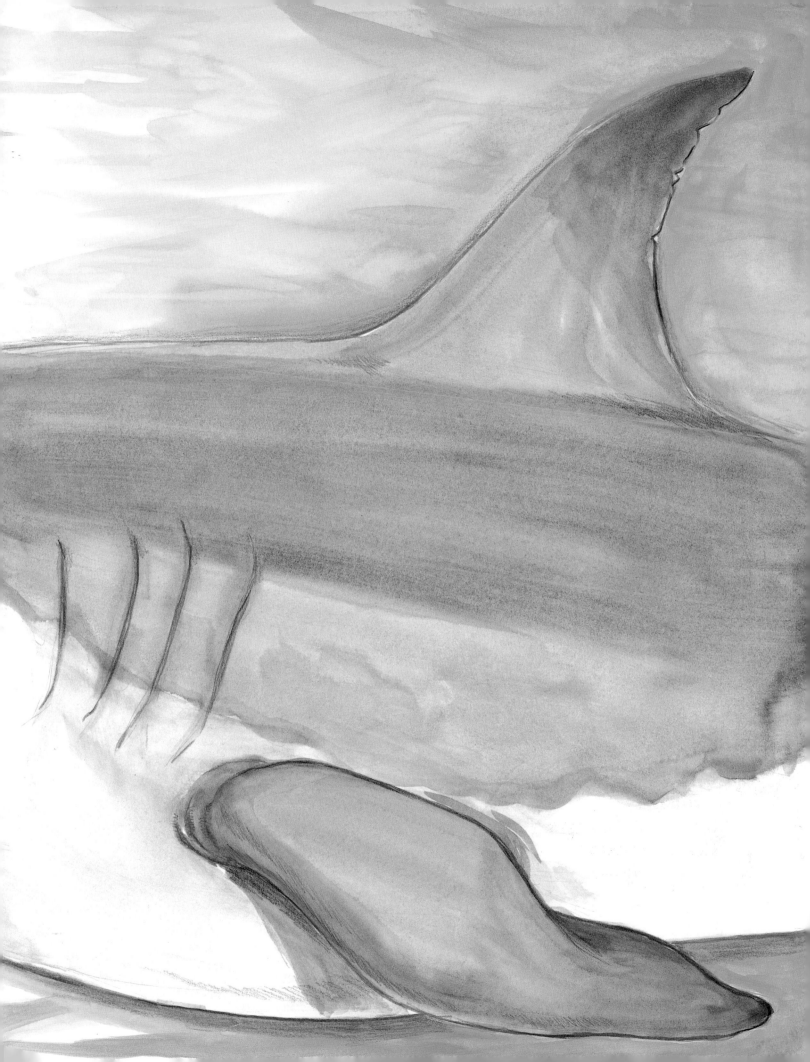

"Mama! Mama! Will you take me fishing?"

"¡Mamá! ¡Mamá! ¿Me llevarías de pesca?"

"I can't, Andy. I have to do this laundry today."

"No puedo, Andy. Tengo que lavar la ropa hoy."

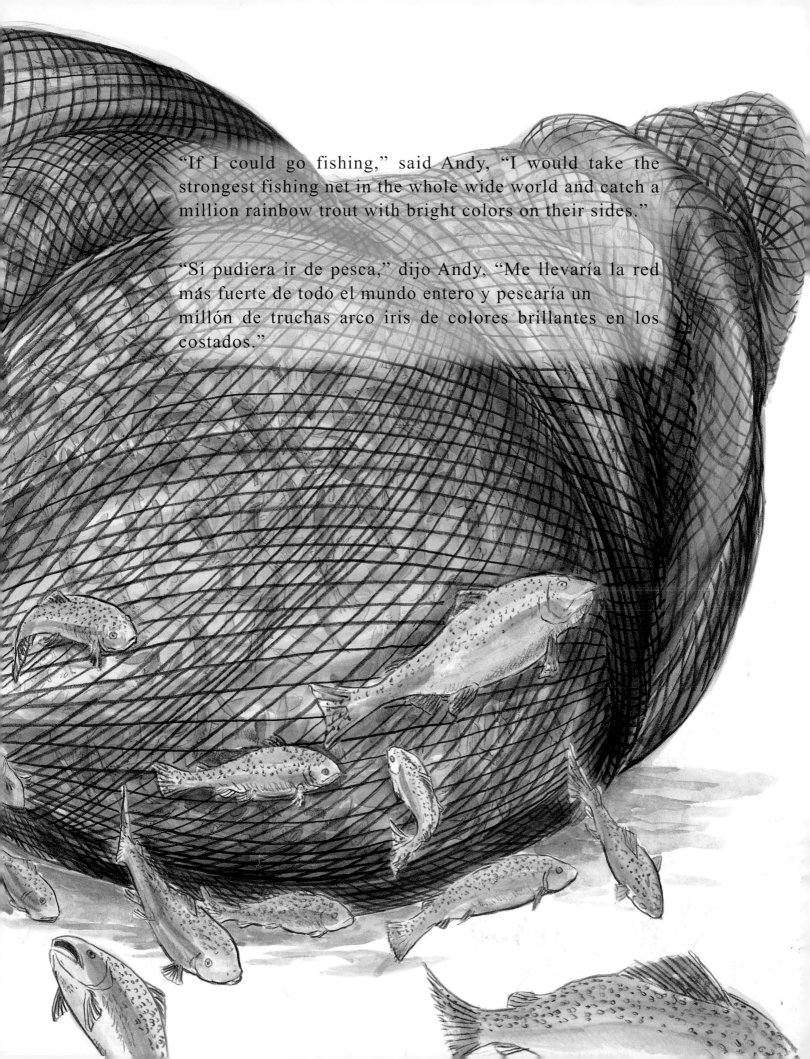

"If I could go fishing," said Andy, "I would take the strongest fishing net in the whole wide world and catch a million rainbow trout with bright colors on their sides."

"Si pudiera ir de pesca," dijo Andy, "Me llevaría la red más fuerte de todo el mundo entero y pescaría un millón de truchas arco iris de colores brillantes en los costados."

"Grandpa! Grandpa! Will you take me fishing?"

"¡Abuelo! ¡Abuelo! ¿Me llevarías de pesca?"

"I'm sorry, Andy, but your Grandma and I have to be at a motorcycle rally for charity. Maybe, when we get back."

"Lo siento, Andy. Tu Abuela y yo tenemos una exhibición de motos para un evento de caridad. A lo mejor, cuando regresemos."

"If I could go fishing," said Andy, "I would use the shiniest lure in the whole wide world to catch a giant swordfish with a long pointed nose."

"Si pudiera ir de pesca," dijo Andy, "usaría el señuelo más brillante de todo el mundo entero y atraparía un pez espada gigante con una larga nariz puntiaguda."

"Tommy! Tommy! Will you take me fishing?"

"¡Tommy! ¡Tommy! ¿Me llevas de pesca?"

"Sorry, Andy. I've got baseball practice this afternoon."

"Lo siento, Andy. Tengo practica de baseball hoy por la tarde."

"If I could go fishing," said Andy, "I would build the best trap in the whole wide world and catch a giant crab with monster claws."

"Si pudiera ir de pesca," dijo Andy, "construiría la mejor trampa de todo el mundo entero y pescaría un cangrejo gigante con unas pinzas monstruosas."

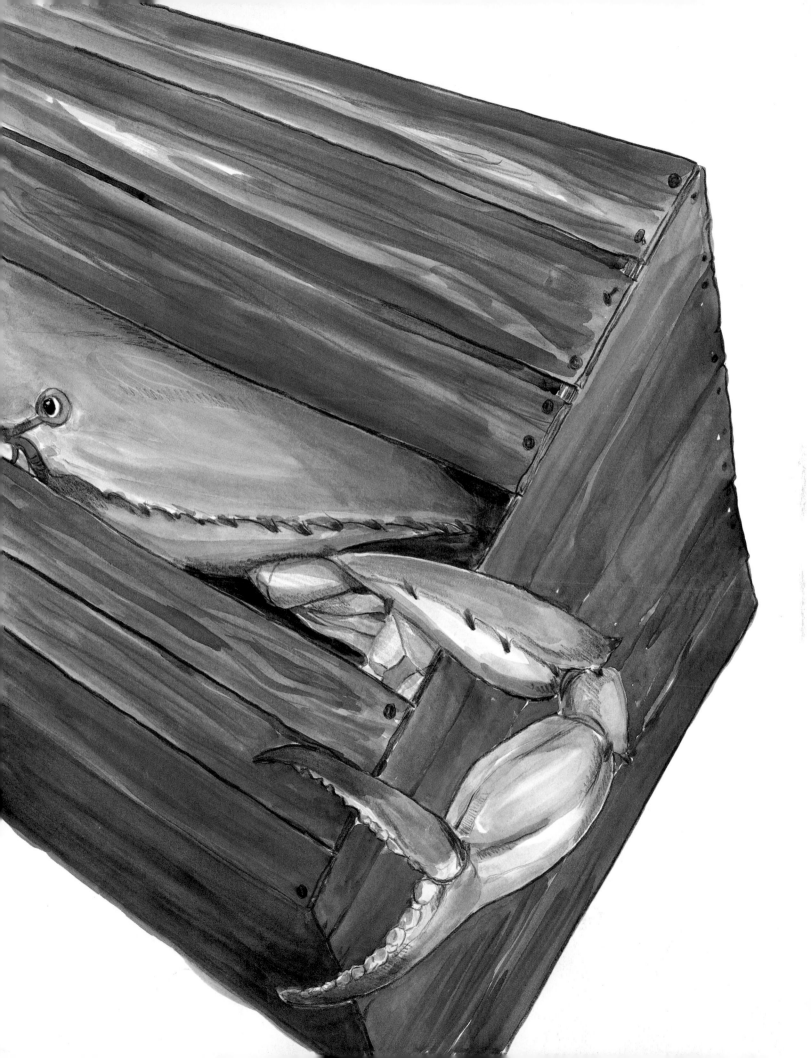

"Tessa! Tessa! Can you take me fishing?

"¡Tessa! ¡Tessa! ¿Me puedes llevar de pesca?"

"Squirt, do I look like I know anything about fishing?
Besides," Tessa said with a shudder, "I hate worms!"

"¿Oye, parezco una persona que sabe de pesca? Además,"
dijo Tessa sintiendo un escalofrío, "¡Odio a las lombrices!"

"I wish I were fishing," said Andy. "Maybe I'll never get to go fishing ever again. Everybody is just too busy."

"Como desearía estar pescando," dijo Andy. "Puede que nunca llegue a ir de pesca. Todos estan tan ocupados."

Andy sat in his room thinking about the amazing fish he could be catching, when he recalled his sister's exact words.

Andy se sentó en su recámara a pensar en los fantásticos peces que podría estar pescando. De repente, se acordó de la palabras exactas que dijo su hermana.

She hadn't really said no.

En realidad ella no había dicho que no podía llevarlo.

Andy jumped up, ran to Tessa's bedroom door, and knocked.

Andy saltó y corrió a la recamara de Tessa. Tocó a la puerta.

He held two fishing poles in one hand and a tackle box in the other.

Andy tomó dos cañas de pescar con una mano y la caja de aperos de pesca, en la otra.

"Tessa!" he announced, "Today is your lucky day. I'm going to teach you how to fish. The first thing you have to know, Sis, is whales don't eat worms!"

"¡Tessa!" exclamó Andy. "¡Hoy es tu día de suerte. Te voy a enseñar a pescar. Y lo primero que debes saber, hermana, es que las ballenas no comen lombrices!"

Author's note:

 Children are our greatest treasure. It is our privilege to love, nurture and teach them.

Nota del Autor:

 Los niños son nuestro mayor tesoro. Es un privilegio amarlos, criarlos y enseñarlos.

Pam Van Scoyoc has always been creative, from dabbling in traditional art to fashion design. In 1993 she began writing for children when she says stories began to pour out of her and has been writing for children ever since.

"I love beautiful art and it is truly art when text and illustrations fit together in a picture book," says Pam. "Children's picture books are magical and I love having a part in producing them."

Other books by Pam: *Angel Wings*, ISBN 0-9663629-1-8 and *The Ballerina With Webbed Feet / La Bailarina Palmípeda*, ISBN 0-9663629-2-6.

Pam Van Scoyoc siempre ha sido una persona muy creativa que ha llevado su creatividad del arte tradicional hasta el diseño de modas. En 1993 ella empezó a crear cuentos para niños en su cabeza y desde entonce no ha parado de escribir para ellos.

"Amo la hermosura del arte y es ahí donde verdaderamente el texto y el arte se conjugan para hacer un libro ilustrado, dice Pam. Los cuentos ilustrados para niños tiene magia y me encanta formar parte de su producción.

Otro libros en Pam: *Angel Wings*, ISBN 0-9663629-1-8 and *The Ballerina With Webbed Feet / La Bailarina Palmípeda*, ISBN 0-9663629-2-6.

R. J. Lewis is a Texas born design consultant, sculptor, animator, airbrush artist and award winning album cover designer. He has attended University of Houston, University of St. Thomas and Rice University in persuit of futhering his art talent. He resides with his wife, Kaylynn, youngest son, Joel and cannine pal, Betty Louise in Cypress, Texas. This is his second book.
He illustrated his first picture book, *The Ballerina With Webbed Feet / La Bailarina Palmípeda*, ISBN 0-9663629-2-6, published by By Grace Enterprises.
His web address is *pristinegraphics@earthlink.net*

R.J. Lewis nacido en Texas, es consultor diseñador, caricaturista, pintor artista ganador de un premio como diseñador de una portada de Albúm. Estudió en las Universidades de Houston, St. Thomas y Rice, persiguiendo siempre mejorar su talento en el arte. Vive con su esposa, Kaylynn, su hijo, Joel y su mascora, Betty Louise, en Cypress, Texas. Este es su segundo libro.
Jason también hizo las ilustraciones de *The Ballerina With Webbed Feet / La Bailarina Palmípeda,* ISBN 0-9663629-2-6, publicado en By Grace Enterprises.
pristinegraphics@earthlink.net

Silvia R. Santillán-Cruz was born in Monterrey, Nuevo Leon, México to Eduardo and Pina, my parents, whom I dearly love. I studied and worked in México. In 2002, I moved to Houston and during October 2004, while being a teacher, I started working as a translator of children's books. I hope everyone enjoys this story as much as I did.

Silvia R. Santillán-Cruz nació en Monterrey, Nuevo León, México siendo mis padres Eduardo y Pina, a quienes amo entrañablemente. Estudió y trabajó en México. En 2002, se fué a Houston a trabajar como maestra y en Octubre del 2004 empezó traduciendo libros para niños. Deseo disfruten de este cuento tanto como yo gozé traduciéndolo.